The
Greatest
SPORTS
QUIZ

Berty Ashley is a molecular biologist with the Dystrophy Annihilation Research Trust and works with rare genetic disorders. What is not rare though is to see him conducting quizzes or attending them. He is the author of the popular *Easy Like Sunday Morning* series of quizzes published in *The Hindu Sunday* magazine. Berty is also a lover of music—not only playing but collecting, as is evident by his growing stack of vinyl records of Jazz, Prog, Hindustani and Heavy metal music. He and his partner, Akhila, live in Bengaluru, surrounded by books, music, and an assortment of pens and guitars.

Akhila Phadnis is a freelance translator. She holds a Masters in Translation Studies from Durham University, UK, and in Psychology from Madras University, Chennai, Tamil Nadu. She enjoys reading, practicing calligraphy, learning new languages, quizzing, board games, and taking long walks by the beach.

The Greatest SPORTS QUIZ

BERTY ASHLEY
AND
AKHILA PHADNIS

RUPA

Published by
Rupa Publications India Pvt. Ltd 2019
7/16, Ansari Road, Daryaganj
New Delhi 110002

Sales centres:
Allahabad Bengaluru Chennai
Hyderabad Jaipur Kathmandu
Kolkata Mumbai

ISBN: 978-93-5333-599-1

First impression 2019

10 9 8 7 6 5 4 3 2 1

The moral right of the author has been asserted.

CONTENTS

INTRODUCTION

The authors are both mad followers of different sports—and usually end up letting their emotions run away with them when following their favourite teams and players. In fact, any passion for watching or following sports basically involves a constant emotional roller coaster. Fierce loyalties to teams and individual players are often supplemented by sheer unpredictability and uncertainty until the very end of any match or contest. Consistent in its power to break your heart or send you home mad with joy, these contests of talent, skill and sheer determination have swayed humans for millenia, in varying forms.

But sports are not just about an individual's loyalties. We have all, at different times, experienced the humble pleasure of watching humans test themselves time and time again. The exhilaration of watching people who are highly skilled at various physical and sporting feats demonstrate their prowess and the incredible versatility of the human body and human mind when they work together, and the uplifting joy of watching multiple people combine these skills in team events is manifold.

Sports are also highly valued in many societies for the qualities of equanimity, discipline and physical fitness that they bring to a player's life. Children across the world play various sports and games in schools, from organized sports with strict rules to games that are made up with new rules every day! Sports are not all serious business—every sport has its light moments and warm sportsmanship. And then there are those games that are crazy combinations of existing games, creatively meshed together, with highly entertaining results and rules.

This book tries to cover all this and more from the world of sports—from asking you for the names of these new, blended sports based on descriptions, to identifying famous sportspeople, to asking you to identify interesting, strange or breathtaking records and achievements. Many answers can be worked out from clues and hints in the questions—we can guarantee that there are at least a few questions in every section that people can answer even if they've never heard of the sport in question before!

We hope that whether as an individual pursuit or a team game, you enjoy cracking the questions posed in this book and learn new facts, revisit old favourites and use them all to come up with your own questions and follow-up questions for people around you. And always remember Kipling's famous lines, golden words for sports and spectators: '*If you can meet* with *Triumph and Disaster/And treat those two impostors just the same...*'

Words to live by—and words you'll meet again in the book, when you come to a particular question!

Happy quizzing...may you always be sporting.

Sports is the toy department of human life.

—Howard Cosell

1. ATHLETICS (TRACK AND FIELD)

1. The 2008 Beijing Olympics Women's 100m sprint winners were unique in two aspects. Firstly, they were all from Jamaica. Shelly-Ann Fraser took the gold with her time of 10.78sec. Her colleagues Sherone Simpson and Kerron Stewart followed her. What was the other unique aspect of the result of that particular race which, as of 2019, has not happened again at the Olympics?

2. As a child, this lady used to chase rabbits to increase her speed. She was a full-time bank teller and part-time beautician and decided to attempt to take part in the Olympics. With every round in the 100m, she constantly clocked better time and her timing in the final was better than all the men in the decathlon. During her run in the 200m race, she broke the world record twice, in the same day. She was known for her flamboyant outfits and coloured nails. Who is this lady who, at that time, was considered to be the fastest woman alive?

3. In athletics, a foot race across a short distance with an all-out or nearly all-out burst of speed has a particular name. The unique feature of these races is that the course for these races is usually marked off in lanes, within which each runner must remain for the entire race—this does not apply to longer races. What is the name of such races, in which the chief distances run are 100, 200 and 400m?

4. The Kalenjin are a semi-nomadic ethnic group inhabiting much of what was the Rift Valley Province in Kenya. They are estimated to number a little over 4.9 million individuals as per the 2009 Kenyan census. Since the mid-1960s, they have been famous for producing superstars in a particular event. From 1980 onwards, about 40 per cent of the top honours available to men at international level competitions in this event have been earned by Kalenjin. One theory as to why this is so is that schools are rare and far from home and there are no modes of transport in these areas. What are the Kalenjin apparently better at than most other people in the world?

5. Fauja Singh was born in Punjab with very weak legs and could not walk long distances. He was an amateur runner but had to give it up after Partition. He emigrated to England in 1994 and started running seriously. On 13 October 2011 he broke 8 world records in one day. Singh broke the records for the 100, 200, 400, 800, 1500, 3000 and 5000m. Some events had no previous record-holder, as nobody in his category

had ever attempted the distance. Three days later, he became the first in his category to finish a marathon. What category in athletics is Fauja Singh, known as the 'Turbaned Tornado', a multiple record-holder in?

6. This is a rare sprint race that was an Olympic event at the 1900 and 1904 Olympics but was removed thereafter. The current men's world record holder is the American Christian Coleman with a time of 6.34sec. During his specialty run at the 2009 World Athletics Championships, Usain Bolt actually beat this world record, but it could not be counted, as the record has to be set during that particular event. What event is this?

7. This country has been participating in the Olympics since 1956. They have won 54 medals overall, of which 22 are gold, 11 are silver and 21 are bronze and, in the process of winning these, they have set one world record and seven Olympic records. The most prolific of these winners was Tirunesh Dibaba. She won three gold and three bronze medals. Interestingly, every single medal won by this country has been in athletics, particularly in the marathon, 10000m, 5000m, 3000m steeplechase and the 1500m. What is the name of this country?

8. Today's modern outdoor track is oval in shape and has eight lanes. The inside lane covers a distance of 400m. However, if you ran all the way around the outermost lane, you would cover about 50m more. So, something had to be done to ensure that every runner covered an

equal distance instead of the outside tracks' runners having to run farther to reach the finish line. This was done by implementing a particular style of starting, where each runner is assigned a lane to run in. The innermost runner will be on the line and each runner from there on starts slightly farther and forward. What is this type of start, which is necessary for an impartial race, known as?

9. This athletic event is a foot race across an obstacle course that has water ditches, open ditches and fences that have to be jumped over as athletes run. The most common distance run is 3000m. The event is supposed to have originated from a race in Ireland where horses and riders would race from one town to another. The church tower and spire, which were visible over long distances, were used as markers of the starting and finishing points. Along the way, the contestants would have to cross streams and low walls. The name of the event comes from the word which refers to the tower and spire of the church and the fact that the contestants run towards it. What is the name of this event?

10. These two Olympic races consist of multiple events such as running, jumping and throwing. The athletes taking part in these events are highly respected as they require speed, strength and, especially, dynamism. The event takes place over two days and they have to maintain a high level of concentration over the entire period. For women, the events are 100-m hurdles,

high jump, shot put, 200m, long jump, javelin and 800m, in that order. For men, the events are 100m, long jump, shot put, high jump, 400m, 110-m hurdles, discus throw, pole vault, javelin and 1500m. What are the names of these two events that correspond to the number of different things each group has to perform?

11. Jonathan Edwards made headlines for the way in which he won a gold medal in his historic performance at the 1995 World Championships held in Sweden. On his first attempt, he became the first man to pass the 18-m barrier in his event with a result of 18.16m. This was a world record, but it stayed for hardly 20 minutes as, in his second attempt, he achieved 18.29m, making him the first ever to get to 60ft, a record that still stands as of 2019. What is the name of this event that requires athletes to hop, bound and jump?

12. This event is a long-distance discipline typically covering 20km and 50km at the Olympics. Usually held on the road, the sport originated from the British sport of pedestrianism which was a type of long-distance competitive walking. The main rule of this event is that one foot must appear to be in contact with the ground at all times. This leads to the peculiar but taxing gait which athletes have during this event. What is the name of this event?

13. This event is known as 'Svenskstafett', referring to the country from which it originated. It has been around since 1910 and, in the country of origin, is it still a national championship event. It soon became popular

in Germany, where it was known as 'Schwedenstaffel'. It is the only relay event on the programme of the World Youth Championships. It is a track event for 4 runners where the first runner runs 100m, the second one 200m, the third 300m and the fourth 400m, so the total length of the race is 1km. The current world record is held by a Jamaican team in which Usain Bolt ran the 200m. What is the name of this event?

14. This athletic event is known as retro running and has championships dedicated to it. This type of running is not energy-efficient but has been known to reduce knee pain. It also requires more coordination and, therefore, develops brain power along with muscle power. Some of the most frequent practitioners of this are referees in football and rugby, allowing them to continuously observe an area of play without interfering with play. How do we better know retro running?

15. This was an athletic event in the Olympics till 1912. The athlete stands on a line marked on the ground with feet slightly apart, takes off and lands using both feet, swinging the arms and bending the knees to provide forward drive. The current world record is 12ft 2in. by American football player Byron Jones. It is one of the physical fitness tests that officer cadets must complete at the Royal Military College of Canada and the United States Air Force Academy. What is the name of this event that gave way to the running long jump?

ANSWERS

1. They tied for silver at 10.98sec. and even a photo finish could not determine who finished ahead, so two silver medals were given with no bronze.

2. Florence Griffith Joyner

3. Sprint

4. Running: from 800m to the marathon, they have won more than any other group of people

5. Centenarian runner (He was a hundred years old in 2011.)

6. 60m sprint

7. Ethiopia

8. Staggered start

9. Steeplechase

10. Heptathlon and decathlon (7 and 10 respectively)

11. Triple jump

12. Racewalking

13. Swedish relay

14. Backward running

15. Standing long/broad jump

2. BALL AND BAT SPORTS

1. This city's Major League baseball team was originally known as Colt .45s but in 1965 their name was changed to Astros. This was done to honour the 'space age capital of the world' the city had become. Consequently, they built the Astrodome' which was the first domed sports stadium in the world. They won their first world series in 2017, beating the LA Dodgers. Which city is the hometown of the aptly named Astros?

2. On 11 March 2010 this company launched its cricket bat in India, with a certain Chennai Super Kings player as the brand ambassador. A former Australian Test player referred to it as 'a half-brick on a stick'. Though it had a longer handle than normal, the size proportion was the same as a normal bat, so it was legal to be used. It facilitated big hitting, which fit the player who was promoting it. It didn't, however, see much action once the player retired from the game. What is the name of this unique bat?

3. In 1893, a bowler bowling a bouncer was unheard-of. At that time, matches usually lasted for two days with two innings on each day. As long as the chasing team didn't lose all their wickets, even if they didn't equal the score of the team batting first, the match was a draw. Moreover, the English at that time followed a 5-ball-over system, unlike the present 6-ball-over. The concept of a no-ball when the front foot crosses the crease was a rule introduced in 1962, which means that during the 1890s there wouldn't be a reason for a no-ball. In which well-known match were these issues present?

4. This sport is a faster variant of baseball, played with a larger ball and in a smaller playing area. The earliest known version of this game supposedly took place on Thanksgiving Day in Chicago between Yale University and Harvard University students. Legend has it that they played with a rolled-up boxing glove as a ball and a broom handle as a bat. The rules were soon put forward to make it suitable for indoor play, so that baseball players could maintain their skills during winter. The main difference between baseball and this game is that the ball is delivered using an underhand motion. The name of this game comes from an earlier version, where the ball used to be made from a material not as hard as the one used for baseball. What is the name of this sport which is played in many colleges?

5. Kilikiti is very popular sport among the people living on islands in the Pacific. The game is said to have

originated from cricket, which was introduced by English missionaries. The game uses a hard rubber ball enveloped in palm leaves and a three-sided war club made from stalks of coconut fronds or the wood from hibiscus. Unlike cricket, there is no restriction on team size, and the bowling alternates between two bowlers at each end of the pitch, which, accordingly, have one wicketkeeper each. This is the national game of an island nation which is found in the Pacific Ocean. In 2001, the inaugural Kilikiti World Cup was held at the nearest big city, Auckland. In which country did this sport originate?

6. Crocker is a team sport often played in British summer camps. During play, the bowler will bowl to try and hit the stumps but can do so at his own pace even if the batsman is not ready. If the batsman hits the ball, he must run either to his left or right around the stump. If the ball touches the body, the batsman is given 'half-out', and if it happens again then the batsman is out. The rules of two games come together to form Crocker. Name these two games.

7. This is a sport that dates back to the fifteenth century in Sussex and is often described as Sussex's 'national' sport. It resembles cricket but gets its name from the legend that it was initially played by milkmaids who used the milk bowl as a bat and a certain item of furniture which they usually carried around with them for the wicket. It is one of the earliest sports in which women participated and, till now, it's mostly played by

women. As it is played today, a bowler attempts to hit the wicket, which is a square piece of wood fastened to a post at shoulder height, and a batswoman defends it using a bat shaped like a frying pan. In 2008 it was officially recognized as a sport by the Sports Council of the UK. What is the name of this sport?

8. This version of baseball was developed by Philip Weidner and was patented in 2010. Unlike the original game, in this, both teams are on the field at the same time. Pitchers from each team take turns pitching to batters at two adjacent home plates. One team runs around the base in a clockwise direction, and the other runs around in a counter-clockwise direction. What is the name of this version of baseball, which puts it on a par with bungee jumping and skydiving?

9. This sport was one of the three demonstration sports which were included in the 1992 Summer Olympics held in Barcelona. The final was won by Argentina, with Spain coming second. It is believed that the sport was included on the insistence of the then IOC president Juan Antonio Samaranch, as he used to play this sport as a child and was even instrumental in setting up the Spanish authority which governed this sport. This sport is also known as Quad and is made up of two five-man teams who try to drive a ball into the opponents' goal with their sticks, while going around on skates. It's a very fast sport which gets its popular name from a combination of the way the players move and the game it most closely resembles. What is the

common name of this sport?

10. This sport is one of the oldest known on record, originating over 2,500 years ago. It is played with just two pieces of equipment, a long wooden stick and a small oval-shaped piece of wood. The teams can number from three or four to even a hundred. The player has to be inside a circle and hit the wood with the stick and run and touch a pre-agreed point outside the circle and return before the piece is retrieved. There is no fixed dimensions of the playing area and limit on the number of players. In some versions, the number of points scored by a striker depends on the distance the wooded piece falls from the striking point. What are the various names that this game is known by in India?

ANSWERS

1. Houston
2. Mngoose
3. The cricket match in the film *Lagaan*
4. Softball
5. Samoa
6. Cricket and baseball
7. Stoolball
8. Extreme baseball
9. Roller hockey
10. Gilli danda (Hindi), dangulli (Bengali), chinni kolu

(Kannada), kuttiyum kolum (Malayalam), vitti dandu (Marathi), kitti pul (Tamil), gooti billa/chirra gonay (Telugu), koyandobal (Konkani) and many more

3. RACQUET SPORTS

1. This is a 2017 American documentary film about famed tennis coach Nick Bollettieri and his troubled relationship with his top player Andre Agassi. It is the story of the coach's relentless desire to win, which cost him his relationships with people he valued the most. The name of the film refers to the fact that relationships mean nothing to him and also refers to a basic rule in the scoring system in tennis. What is the name of the documentary?

2. A study by the *British Journal of Sports Medicine*, which examined the link between various sports and the risk of early death, identified racquet sports as the best sport for helping live a longer life (a simplified summary of the results). This may be explained by a kind of movement that racquet sports offer that other sports typically do not. This particular kind or direction of movement results in improved balance and weight-shifting which may lower the risk of falls. It

was also found that the sport offered cognitive benefits from having to plan and think ahead for the next shot to play. What is this physical movement offered by racquet sports and not by most others?

3. Badminton has one very specific requirement with respect to the components of the shuttlecock. Competition shuttlecocks are always made of feathers: 16 feathers inserted into a cork base. However, these 16 feathers come from a very specific set of feathers. While it may be seen as a quirk of the sport, there is actually a scientific reason behind this. The curvature of these particular feathers prevents the shuttlecock from wobbling and also ensures that it spins clockwise. Other feathers would make it spin in an counter-clockwise direction (potential to cause chaos in the game) and a mix of feathers would cause a wobble, which is highly undesirable. What specific set of feathers do these 16 feathers come from?

4. This game, commonly known today as 'real tennis' or 'court tennis', was developed in the eleventh and twelfth centuries and was played by hitting a ball using the hands, returning it to another player and bouncing the ball off surfaces around the player. As cities and towns grew crowded, the game moved on to dedicated courts. It was called *jeu de paume* (*jeu*: game, *paume*: palm) in French, a name that continues to be used, although racquets became a standard feature by the seventeenth century. There is a *jeu de paume* court at the Palace of Versailles and in 1789, when they were

locked out of the main meeting hall, representatives of the common people, along with certain representatives of the clergy and nobility met on this court and took an oath to give their country a constitution. What famous event in French history can be traced back to this meeting?

5. This gentleman is one of the most successful coaches in tennis but started off in table tennis, where he was a junior champion. His younger brother Miguel was a professional footballer who played with FC Barcelona and his other brother was called Sebastian. He introduced Sebastian's three-year-old son to tennis. The child was actually right-handed, but his uncle started coaching him and made him play left-handed as this provided a natural advantage on a tennis court. The nephew went on to be the first and only left-hander (as of 2019) to win 4 Grand Slam titles and holds longest winning streak on clay courts. Name this uncle-nephew duo whose names have been cemented in the history of tennis.

6. This sport, which *Forbes* magazine declared as being the healthiest sport to play, is thought to have originated in Fleet Street prison, when prisoners used to hit balls off the walls with racquets, leading to the game 'racquets'. This was then adapted by schoolboys at Harrow School, who used a punctured 'racquets' ball and discovered that this ball flattened on impact and bounced off, leading to a greater variety of possible shots. It is believed that the name of this sport

comes from the sound of this impact or the thing that happens to the ball on impact against the wall. What is the name of this sport?

7. The All England Open Badminton Championships is one of the most prestigious in the sport. In 1980, an Indian badminton player became the first Indian player to win this tournament. This win, along with multiple other successes around the year, also led to their becoming the first Indian to achieve another sporting goal in badminton. This player then returned to India and set up a badminton academy that trained another badminton star, Pullela Gopichand, who in turn then coached P.V. Sindhu, who has won multiple laurels in her sport. Who is this player who in every way possible, as a player and as the head of this academy, has truly put India on the world map?

8. This iconic tennis player had become a table tennis World Champion at the age of twenty, before switching to tennis, a sport he also went on to dominate. Apart from being a three-time Wimbledon champion, winning in three consecutive years, he was also the first male tennis player to hold all 4 Grand Slam titles at the same time (though he did not win them in the same year). He won a total of 8 Grand Slams in his career, a phenomenal achievement by any measure. He played a key role in Britain's Davis Cup victory, though he later moved to the United States (US) as he faced a lot of discrimination and disapproval in the United Kingdom (UK) because of his 'working

class' roots. He did later reconcile with the British sporting world, which honoured him by erecting his statue at Wimbledon and naming one of the gates there after him. He set up his own sportswear brand and continued to follow tennis avidly after retirement, working as a tennis commentator. Fittingly, perhaps, he passed away in Melbourne in 1995, where he was attending the Australian Open. Who is this legendary tennis player?

9. The Tournament of Champions is believed to be the 'oldest annual tournament for squash professionals' and its history can be traced back to the 1930s. It is one of the biggest tournaments in the sport and attracts large crowds. It first took place at an iconic landmark in this city in 1999 and this has now become the home of the tournament. What is the name of this unusual spot, which may be thought of as a 'training' ground, and in which city is it located?

10. This sport can be traced back to India, China and ancient Greece, where different variations of it were played. British soldiers posted in India earlier knew this game as poona. However, today this sport is named after the country estate of the Duke of Beaufort in England, where it was played by soldiers in 1837. There is a unique entity used in this sport that came into existence in this house because its light weight would not cause damage to the life-sized portraits of horses that were hung around the great hall. The sport became the fastest racquet sport in the world, with

the object being hit moving as fast as 200mph and top players covering as much as 4 miles in a single match. What is the name of the house of the Duke of Beaufort and, consequently, what is the name of the sport?

11. This squash player is widely considered to be among the greatest of all times, winning 6 World Championships and 10 British Open titles. His brother, also a squash player, died of a heart attack during a game and he initially wanted to give up on the game following this incident. But he continued as a tribute to his brother and, at the peak of his prowess, had a five-year-eight-month-long winning streak. Who was this magnificent player and which country did he come from, which has a history of producing some of the greatest squash players?

12. This tennis player began playing tennis at the age of four and won the Czechoslovakia national tennis championship at fifteen. At the age of nineteen, the player defected to the US and became a citizen there. This player went on to win 59 major titles (18 Grand Slam singles, 31 Grand Slam doubles and 10 Grand Slam mixed doubles), also winning 369 titles overall in their career, including a record (as of 2019) 9 Wimbledon titles. Apart from the phenomenal successes on the court, this player also had a tremendous social impact, being one of the first openly gay athletes in tennis, helping fight against prejudice and discrimination. Who is this trailblazing tennis star and activist?

13. Toccer is a sport where two teams of ten players

compete against each other on a football field. The sport is played with tennis balls and a goal is scored by throwing a tennis ball into a goal which is defended by a goalkeeper who can deflect the ball only with a racquet. In another variation of the game, all the other players use racquets as well. This fast-paced sport is also known by another name which combines the two sports from which the equipment and rules are taken. What is this name by which toccer is also known?

14. Esther Vergeer was a top-ranked player in her sport and had a fantastic career until she retired in 2013, with a 470-match winning streak, a figure that is second across all top-level sports only to one of the best squash players of all time (this figure may now be revised taking into account fresh calculations in the squash player's career). She has won 21 major singles titles and, when she retired, the last match she had lost was in 2003! What sport did this incredible player play?

15. In 1974, India reached its second-ever Davis Cup finals and was a strong contender for the title, with Jasjit Singh, Vijay Amritraj and Anand Amritraj forming the main team. However, India forfeited the title by refusing to play their opponents as a protest against a certain policy practiced by that country. Who were these opponents and against what practice did the Indian team take a strong and proud stance?

ANSWERS

1. *Love Means Zero*
2. Lateral or side-to-side movement
3. The left wing of a goose
4. The French Revolution
5. Toni Nadal (uncle) and Rafael Nadal (nephew)
6. Squash
7. Prakash Padukone
8. Fred Perry (Frederick John Perry)
9. Grand Central Terminal, New York
10. Badminton House, badminton
11. Jehangir Khan, Pakistan
12. Martina Navratilova
13. Tennis polo
14. Wheelchair tennis
15. South Africa, apartheid

4. TEAM NAMES

1. This basketball team was set up in 1974, and they named themselves after the most famous cultural aspect of the city. The name also meant 'collective improvisation'. In 1979, the franchise was sinking, so it was decided to move it to Salt Lake City. Unfortunately, the new city was not known for that particular cultural aspect, and it was too late to receive league approval for a change of name before the season, hence the name, though not fitting, stayed. Which basketball team is this which is yet to win a Championship title?

2. This peculiar name of this short-lived IPL team was actually in the plural in the first season that they played. In the second season, they removed the 's' at the end of their name and became singular. This, according to the team, was done to project the image of a unified team, rather than that of a group of players. Another interesting observation made about the four-word name was that if it was abbreviated, the

letters would correspond to the name of the entity that owned the franchise, RP-Sanjiv Goenka Group. What is the name of this IPL team which lost the last game they ever played by just one run?

3. This is the basketball team of the city of San Antonio in Texas. With 5 championships won, they have a high winning percentage among active NBA teams. They initially started out as the Dallas Chapparrals which is a reference to the type of vegetation found in the area. They moved to San Antonio and took on the name Gunslingers, but that name did not last. They changed their name to the present one, which refers to an integral part of a cowboy's wardrobe and also means 'to encourage or prompt someone on'. What is the name of this basketball team?

4. This IPL team had a long history of underperforming in the IPL and was the only team from the original few who never made it to the final of any edition of the IPL. As a makeover for the team, they changed their name and got a new logo. The new name refers to the city that they are based out of, which is the power centre of the country, and the logo is inspired by the design of one of the most iconic buildings in the city. Which IPL team is this and which building is referred to in the logo?

5. This basketball team is one of the most successful teams in NBA history, having won 17 championships. From 1959 to 1966, they won a record 8 consecutive championship titles, a streak which remains unbeaten.

The name of the team and their mascot is a nod to the city's historically large Irish population. Which team is this that, as of 2019, has yet to win a championship since 2008?

6. Most people believe that this baseball team gets its name from the cunning tricks one would use to avoid a tag or steal a base. However, the name actually refers to a certain activity practised in Brooklyn from the late 1800s, when people had to move fast to avoid being run over by fast-moving trolley cars that were powered by the then new invention called electricity. The pedestrians hadn't learned the habit of looking both ways before crossing a road because they knew that if a horse were to come, it would just stop. Unfortunately, these trolleys did not stop in a similar way, hence they had to make these moves. This baseball team, which originated in Brooklyn but later moved west, derives its name from this practice. What is the name of this team?

7. The Badminton Association of India introduced a new team for the fourth edition of the Indian Badminton League in 2018, owned by Bollywood actress Taapsee Pannu and KRI entertainment. they are based out of Pune and are led by Olympic and three-time world champion Carolina Marín. The name of the franchise is a combination of a number that the Greeks and the Egyptians used to denote completion, and the term used to refer to a serve that is untouchable. What is the name of the newest entrant to the Indian Badminton League?

8. This American football team is based out of Cincinnati but has a name that has a connection to the Indian subcontinent. One theory is that the name comes about as a tribute to a rare white version of a big cat which was in the world-renowned zoo in the city. The name of the team is a direct reference to the area in which this particular species was usually found. The team's colour, though, is the characteristic black and orange of the cat. What is the name of this team?

9. This team led by Dilip Tirkey (who also captained the national hockey team) won the Premier Hockey League in 2007. Their name was originally Rourkela 'X', referring to the city being the hockey capital of the state and also the fact that it has one of the largest plants of SAIL. The name also refers to the main product Rourkela is known for and also to the fact that the hockey team could take away the ball from the opponent without them noticing it. Now named after the state, what is the name of this team?

10. This American basketball team is a rare team that has a number for a name. They have won three championships and have been the home of many players who have gone on to become legends in the sport. Earlier known as the 'Nationals', a contest was held to decide their new name after they relocated to their current home. The winning name referred to the fact that the United States Declaration of Independence was signed in that city in that particular year. What is the name of this team which has a very patriotic-looking logo?

ANSWERS

1. Utah Jazz
2. Rising Pune Super Giant
3. San Antonio Spurs
4. Delhi Capital, the Parliament building
5. Boston Celtics
6. Los Angeles Dodgers
7. Pune 7 Aces
8. Cincinnati Bengals
9. Orissa Steelers
10. Philadelphia 76ers

5. ROUND BALL SPORTS

1. In 1920, a leading sports magazine wrote a letter to the governing body of a particular sport with a suggestion that a team of 12-20 American professionals be chosen to play in England as, till then, no American had ever won at it. They suggested a warm-up tournament two weeks prior to the actual tournament and they got a wealthy businessman to sponsor it, naming the tournament after him. This led to the creation of a now-famous biennial tournament in that sport which alternates between British and US venues. Name the sport and the tournament.

2. Nine minutes into a game, a Newcastle winger awkwardly bounced a ball to Peter Lovenkrands who quickly netted it. This brought an end to an impressive feat, as the person who let it slip past had enjoyed a 1311-minute record which stood from 15 November 2008 to 21 February 2009. Who is this person who, for more than 20 hours of play, had not conceded a single

goal, and which team did he play for?

3. The top 5 batsmen in this list are 3 Sri Lankans and 2 Pakistanis. Muttiah Muralitharan has 25, Mahela Jayawardene and Wasim Akram each have 28, Shahid Afridi has 30 and leading the list is Sanath Jayasuriya with 34. What not-so-illustrious list is this, which has such iconic sportsmen?

4. Only two football coaches have the holy trinity of all three major European club titles: UEFA Champions League, UEFA Europa League, UEFA Winners' Cup. One of them is Giovanni Trapattaoni, who won all three with the team Juventus. The other one has coached Franz Beckenbauer, Lothar Matthäus, Bernd Schuster and Diego Maradona, whom he once left behind because he didn't make it to the team bus on time. Who is this legendary coach?

5. This annual football match is featured at number four on the *Financial Times* list of 'Great college sports rivalries' in the UK. The teams that contest are the Department of Peace Studies of the University of Bradford and the Department of War Studies of King's College London, both being academic, regional and ideological rivals. The former holds the overall edge with 7 trophies to the latter's 2. The rolling trophy came into existence in 2007 and is kept for a year by the winners. The original trophy was retired after the 2011 edition because of its fragile state and was replaced with a new one. Name the tournament and say what the trophy is.

6. In 1989, Geet Sethi became the only person in the history of his sport to have two independent world records in two separate versions of his sport. He scored a maximum (147) in a game of the first version of the sport in Guntur and a 1000+ break in competition in the other version. What are these two sports which laymen routinely mistake for each other?

7. Between 2003 and 2004, this English Premier League team went undefeated for a total of 49 league games, till they lost in a match known as the 'Battle of the Buffet', against opponents Manchester United at Old Trafford. A series of unprofessional fouls were overlooked and Wayne Rooney was given a controversial penalty which Van Nistelrooy converted. The team was deprived of a chance of making it to 50 undefeated games when Rooney scored a second goal later. What is the name of this team which, having been relegated only once in 1913, has been on the longest streak in the top division?

8. This is a variant of football which is played on an indoor hard court between teams of 5 players each, in a field smaller than a regular football field. The game's emphasis is on improvisation, creativity and technique. The name comes from the shortening of the phrase in Spanish for 'hall football'. The sport was invented by a Uruguayan teacher, for playing in the YMCA, after the country had won the 1930 World Cup. He based it on football but took some rules from other sports, such as 5 players per team (basketball), goalkeeper's rules

(water polo) and field and goal size (handball). What is the name of this game?

9. This is a game which was created in 1965 in Brazil, combining the field rules of beach volleyball and the ball-touch rules of football. The sport started in Rio de Janeiro apparently because football was banned on the beach, but volleyball courts were open. The game is essentially beach volleyball where players do not use their hands, and a football replaces the volleyball. The name of the sport comes from the first words of the parent sports. What is the name of this sport?

10. Palant is a game similar to baseball, played with a wooden stick which is about 60-80cm in length. It has a peculiar concept of 'heaven' and 'hell', which are the two playing fields. The team in 'hell' plays to obtain 'heaven' by trying to catch the ball as soon as possible from the players in 'heaven', who bounce the ball behind the designated line with a wooden stick. The game is thought to have originated with immigrants from a certain country, who arrived in 1609 with Captain John Smith to serve in industries in Jamestown Colony. From which country did these skilled artisans come, bringing their game of palant with them?

11. This is a sport in which players use their hands to hit a small rubber ball against a wall, such that their opponent cannot do the same without it touching the ground twice. Many versions of this sport have been recorded throughout history, with the furthest going

back to the Aztecs. King James I of Scotland was supposed to have played this in 1427. Squash and racquetball were heavily influenced by this sport and were essentially created when people started using paddles or racquets to play this sport. What is the very simple name of this historic sport?

12. George Best, Denis Law and Sir Bobby Charlton were the three players who, in 1968, helped Manchester United become the first ever English football club to win the European Cup. All three won the Ballon d'Or for being the world's best football player in the 1960s. Between themselves, they scored 665 goals in 1633 games. There is a statue outside Old Trafford which depicts the three of them. By what divine sounding name are they referred to?

13. Boxla is an indoor version of this sport that was first played in Canada in the 1930s. It is played between two teams of five players and one goalie each. It is usually played on ice hockey rinks after the ice has been removed or has been covered. In the original sport, the athletes carry a stick that has a net at the end to catch and pass a ball which is then put into a goal to score points. This is done a field, but Boxla is played in a closed area called 'X'. The name of the sport is a combination of the name of the area and the original sport it evolved from. What is the full form of boxla?

14. Bandy is a form of hockey which is played with certain rules from soccer, such as two halves of 45 minutes

each and 11 players in each team. As in hockey, the players use a small ball and bowed sticks. The country of its origin is not clear, but there is evidence of it having been played in Russia. The name of this sport comes from 'bander' which is Middle French for 'to strike back and forth' and also refers to the bowed stick. Known as winter football, what surface is bandy played on?

15. This sport is an extremely fast game on grass. It is played with teams of 15 players on a rectangular field with H-shaped goals at each end. One of the earliest references to it has been in Gaelic culture. The sport is named after the wooden stick made of ash wood which is used to hit a small ball, called a sliotar, between the goalposts. The ball can be caught in the hand but not carried for more than 4 steps. It can be kicked or slapped with an open hand. It can be carried for more than 4 steps only by bouncing it on the end of the stick. What is the name of this historic sport?

ANSWERS

1. Ryder Cup
2. Edwin van der Sar, Manchester United
3. Most ducks in their career
4. Udo Lattek
5. Tolstoy Cup, framed copy of *War and Peace*
6. Snooker and billiards

7. Arsenal

8. Futsal

9. Footvolley

10. Poland

11. Handball

12. Holy Trinity or United Trinity

13. Box lacrosse

14. Ice

15. Hurling

6. MOTORSPORTS

1. Marlboro, a long-time sponsor of his team, coined the nickname of this sportsperson, owing to his resemblance to something. When he retired from his sport and started an airline company, it became one of its mascots and was named after him. Who is the sportsperson and what was his nickname?

2. Camber is the vertical tilt of a wheel if you're looking at it from the front or rear of the car. A wheel has zero or neutral camber if it's perfectly perpendicular to the level ground. If the top of a wheel is tilted outwards from the vehicle and the bottom slopes in, the wheel has positive camber. Conversely, if the top of the wheel is tilted towards the vehicle and the bottom slopes outwards, it has negative camber. In this particular motorsport, the cars are designed with negative camber for the right wheels and positive camber for the left wheels. This is because the cars make only left turns and the right wheels will always be on the

outside of a turn. With this combination, these cars have optimal grip and stability during a turn, hence maximizing cornering speeds. Which race is this that has drivers taking these turns at more than 300km/hr?

3. Graeme Obree is a road bicycle racer who races against the clock. He lives in Scotland and suffered from bipolar disorder which led to him trying to commit suicide twice. He ran a bike shop that failed. To combat his problems, he decided to try and beat the World Hour Velodrome record, which was a distance of 51.15km cycled in one hour. He built his own cycle which also had bearings from a washing machine, and named it Old Faithful. Since he had no prior experience in building bikes, his design was very unique and also meant he had a very unusual riding position. After failing by a kilometre on his first try, he returned the very next day (after a night of almost no sleep) and set a new record, beating the old one by 445m. He went on to regain the record again, win the British 10-mile individual time trial and the 50-mile RTTC Championship. He was given a nickname, which he also used as the title of his autobiography, that refers to a famous express passenger train service that runs between Edinburgh and London. What name is Obree known by?

4. Regarded as the greatest in his sport, he is the only person to have won seven world championships of which five were consecutive. He is statistically the best, with multiple records of most wins, fastest times

and most wins in a single season. He is known as Regenkonig (rain king) or Regenmeister (rain master) because of his race-winning performances in wet conditions. He single-handedly made his team into the most valuable brand in the sport. Who is this outstanding athlete whose son made his debut in the same team as his father in March 2019?

5. This particular item in a normal car usually does only one job and in modern cars might have three or four more functions. In a Formula One car, it is fine-tuned and custom-designed for every driver. Using it, a driver can change gears, apply a revolution limiter, adjust the fuel-air mix, change brake pressure and call the radio. There is also a LCD screen that shows engine rpm, lap times, speed and gear. It is made of carbon fibre and is designed to be removed every single time the driver has to exit or enter the car. What is this highly functional hi-tech object?

6. This athlete is the first and (as of 2019) the only rider in the history of his sport to have won the World Championship in four different classes: 125cc, 250cc, 500cc and MotoGP. He has won 9 titles overall. He has very peculiar pre-race rituals such as tightening his boots before he gets on the bike and then spending some time talking to the bike. He has a unique nickname which has many different stories about its origin. According to one story, he was given this title because high-ranking people in Italy are given this. Another time in an interview he stated that the

reason for his surname is that it a common one for that profession. Who is this rider and what is his nickname?

7. This driver was known for his extraordinarily quick reflexes and his fantastic peripheral vision which helped him achieve a record 5 consecutive wins at the very demanding Monaco Grand Prix. Once, as part of a safety-check procedure while going around a circuit near Bologna, he saw a retaining wall. While climbing a partition, he remarked to his teammate Gerhard Berger that since it wasn't possible to move the wall back, it would be very dangerous and it might lead to a fatality. Five years later in a race on the very same track, this brilliant driver had a tragic accident. Who was this iconic driver who is considered by many as one of the greatest drivers of all time?

8. This is a class of motorsports which started in Beijing in 2014, using only environmentally-friendly electric-powered cars. The races usually take place in city-centre street circuits. The concept came about after Jean Todt, the president of the FIA, and Italian politician Antonio Tajani talked about electrification of the automobile industry to reduce carbon dioxide emissions. What is the name of this motorsport which refers to the defining characteristic of this event?

9. In motorsports, there are two main classifications for racing cars. The first one is for cars that have wheels outside the car's main body and have only one seat. These cars usually have low road clearance and have a high degree of technological sophistication. They

are usually not road legal. The second one is for cars where the wheels do not stick outside the bodywork and which usually are multiple seaters. They can race on road as in stock car racing (NASCAR) or off-road racing. What are these two classifications of motorsport?

10. This British automotive company was founded by Bruce _____. Bruce learnt engineering and about cars when he used to hang around his parents' service station in New Zealand. He won his first race by racing an Austin 7 Ulster up a local hill. He moved to the UK and at 22 became the youngest-ever winner of a Grand Prix when he won the US Grand Prix. In 1964, his motor racing company built a race car which raced in the Can-Am Championships and earned 43 victories. Eventually, they entered F1 and went on to win 8 championships and 12 drivers' championships. What is the name of this team that also makes a series of hyper-cars?

ANSWERS

1. Nicki Lauda, rat
2. NASCAR racing
3. The flying Scotsman
4. Michael Schumacher
5. The steering wheel
6. Valentino Rossi, the doctor

7. Ayrton Senna

8. Formula E

9. Enclosed wheel and open wheel

10. McLaren

7. AQUATIC SPORTS

1. This sport is basically an 'aquatized' version of a popular sport which is played by two teams of 6 players each (5 players and 1 goalkeeper). The water version of this sport involves players equipped with snorkels, flippers and thick gloves to protect their hands, free-diving and chasing a flat disc along the floor of a swimming pool. The disc is made of lead and coated with plastic to ensure it can be pushed around but does not float. The name of this sport is a pretty straightforward description of what it is, describing where it is played and the sport it is based on. What is this sport?

2. The Bay of Zea, off the coast of Greece, was once a large Athenian port. In 1896, it made history for a very different reason, one that carried forward an ancient Greek tradition. Which specific sporting event ties the Bay of Zea to the River Seine in Paris?

3. Johnny Weismuller was an incredible athlete, winning five gold medals and one bronze medal at the Olympics. In 1924, at the Paris Olympic Games, he won three gold medals (100m freestyle, 400m freestyle and 2x400m relay team event) as well as a bronze in the water polo competition. At the 1928 Games in Amsterdam, he won gold in the 100m freestyle as well as the 2x400m relay team event. He set 28 world records in swimming and is still regarded as among the greatest swimmers in history. One day, he was swimming in a pool in the Hollywood Athletics Club on Sunset Boulevard, when he caught the eye of a screenwriter, Cyril Hume, who was on the lookout for a man who could portray a character in a film he was working on. Weismuller went on to become the most iconic face of this character, playing him in films between 1932 and 1948. What character was this?

4. Australian swimmer Dawn Fraser is among the greats of the aquatic sports world, winning eight medals across three Olympic Games! However, the Tokyo Olympics of 1964 were eventually her last Olympics. During a party celebrating the end of the Games and the Australian victories, she and two others embarked on a crime quite common to the Olympic Games. However, things went wrong and she was chased by police in Tokyo and injured her leg while trying to escape. When the police caught her they refused to believe, at first, that she was the celebrated swimmer! When her identity was established, she was released so that she could carry the flag in the closing ceremony

the next morning. She was also presented with the object she had been trying to steal. Unfortunately, Australian sports authorities were far stricter and issued a ten-year ban, effectively ending her career. What was this precious object that had led to such high drama?

5. In this sport, individual events are scored by a panel of seven judges who recommend a score between 0 (completely failed) and 10 (excellent). The two highest scores and the two lowest scores are discarded; the remaining three scores are added and multiplied by a difficulty rating. The four main criteria for a judge to watch out for are Approach, Take off, Flight and Entry. For synchronized events, there are 11 judges. Which Olympic event is this?

6. This is a competitive team sport which involves two teams of 6 players and a goalkeeper who try to get a ball into the opponent's goal. All players except the goalkeeper play both defensive and offensive positions. The sport is believed to have originated in Scotland as a version of rugby played in a swimming pool. The most famous (or infamous) match of this sport was the 1956 Melbourne Olympics semifinal between Hungary and the Soviet Union. Just before the start of the match, the Hungarian Revolution had begun but had been crushed by the Soviet army. In the match, the Hungarians won 4-0 but the match was stopped at the last minute to prevent hostility. Which sport is this?

7. This athlete is the most decorated swimmer of all time. When he was just 10, he made a national record and qualified for the 2000 Olympics at 15. In 2003, he made 5 world records at the World Championships. In 2008, he became the first person to win 8 gold medals at a single Olympic Games. He finished his career with a record of 23 Olympic golds, making him the most successful Olympian of all time. Who is this prolific swimmer?

8. At the 2008 Olympics, a controversy was generated when it was found that 94 per cent of all medals awarded in the swimming category had been won by athletes wearing a certain product. Certain critics claimed that the design of the product gave its wearers an unfair advantage, although its manufacturers pointed out that there had always been advances made in what athletes used and the performance put in was entirely down to the athletes. This product was supposed to hug the body 70 times tighter than other products in the market and also helped with core stability. While a new piece was quite expensive, the manufacturer gave away free samples to any swimmer who wanted it at the 2008 Olympics and reported that several of their competitors' clients had also taken one. What was this controversial suit and who were its manufacturers?

9. This word is derived from a seventeenth century Venetian word meaning 'contest' or 'fight' and is used to describe a certain competitive sport that takes place on multiple routes around the world. One of

the most famous of these is the Henley Royal _____, taking place on the River Thames, in England. Another famous example is the Antigua Sailing Week, which attracts the keenest practitioners of the sport. What is this word, usually applied to any large, competitive gathering of sailing or rowing vessels?

10. Hank McGregor is a ten-time Marathon World Champion in a certain sport. The South African announced in 2018 that he was done with the marathon version of the sport and would be retiring after honouring a commitment made to his teammate to finish the International Sella Descent (the Sella is a river). This is a famous sporting event in Spain that dates back to 1929. This competition starts in the town of Arriondas and finishes in Ribadesella. What is the means of descending the Sella and, consequently, in what sport is Hank McGregor a legend?

11. This sport dates back to pre-modern Hawaii and Polynesia. It was revived in the twentieth century, after dying away following the advent of European missionaries who denounced the sport since it was practised by both men and women. The American writer Jack London played a huge part in popularizing this sport after visiting Hawaii. One of the most famous practitioners of the sport, and an Olympic champion, Duke Kahanamoku, demonstrated his skills in Sydney in 1914 and 1915 and this resulted in this sport being widely adopted in Australia, where it remains highly popular to this day. What is this wonderful sport?

12. In this sport, two teams of six players each try to shoot a ball filled with seawater (negatively buoyant) into an opponent's goal at the bottom of a swimming pool. The sport originated from physical fitness training routines that were conducted by German diving clubs. There are six substitutes on hand as it is a fast and exhausting sport in which substitution is quick and aplenty. One of the major rules of this sport is that the ball never leaves the water. The name of the sport is shared with a full-contact English sport which uses a pear-shaped ball with which it shares no features. What is the name of this sport?

13. This is a sport consisting of four techniques, involving swimming with the use of fins either on the surface of the water or under water. It differs from normal swimming because of the use of masks, fins, snorkels and underwater breathing apparatus which comes from the sport's origins in the world of scuba diving. It was demonstrated at the 2015 European Games. One of the major attractions of this sport is the speed which a swimmer can attain. The world record for this event for 50m is 13.85sec., which is seven seconds faster than the record in normal swimming. The name of this sport comes from the usage of a certain item which differentiates it from normal swimming. What is the name of this sport?

14. This sport was developed in France in the 1980s, where it was known as 'Tir sur cible subaquatique'. It tests a competitor's ability to accurately use a speargun, via

a set of individual and team events conducted in a swimming pool. The competitor aims to hit a target without the use of telescopic sights or laser sights. What is the name of this sport which had a World Championship in 1999?

15. Sub-aqua ice hockey is an extreme version of ice hockey. Athletes wear diving masks, fins and wetsuits, and play with a puck and sticks. There are four divers with oxygen tanks at all times, to help players who get disoriented. One of the most important precautions taken is that before every game, a rescue diver uses a chainsaw to cut holes in the rink, located perpendicular to the nets. Athletes should have good breathing skills as they have to stay under water for up to 60sec. What is used as the surface for this sport and how do the athletes play?

ANSWERS

1. Underwater hockey
2. The sites of the swimming races at the first and second Olympic Games
3. Tarzan
4. The Olympic flag
5. Diving
6. Water polo
7. Michael Phelps
8. Speedo's LZR Racer

9. Regatta

10. The canoe, Canoe Marathon

11. Surfing

12. Underwater rugby

13. Finswimming

14. Underwater target shooting

15. The underside of an ice rink, the athletes play upside down

8. COMBAT SPORTS

1. This is a martial art which later evolved into a sport because of its competitive element, where the objective is to either throw an opponent to the ground or force one to submit. The central principles of this system are 'maximum efficiency, minimum effort' and 'mutual welfare and benefit'. This sport was seen for the first time at the Olympic Games in an informal demonstration at the 1932 Los Angeles Games. It became an Olympic sport at the 1964 Tokyo Olympics. The name of this art form means 'gentle way' in Japanese. What is its name?

2. Pankration (Greek for 'all force') was a combination of wrestling and boxing in which almost everything was permitted and it was supposed to have been the method used by Theseus to defeat the Minotaur. From 200 BCE onwards, for 1200 years, pankration was a huge crowd-puller at the Olympics. Nowadays, one can see it in the form of MMA (mixed martial

arts). The only rule during combat was that one was not allowed to stab an opponent's eyes or private parts, but in a particular place in ancient Greece, even that was allowed. In which ancient city, known for its fearless warriors, was this extreme version of pankration practised?

3. John Sholto Douglas was a Scottish nobleman who was the ninth Marquess of Queensberry. In 1866, he founded the Amateur Athletic Club, and in the following year the club published a set of twelve rules for conducting a certain sport. The rules were established by John Graham Chambers who was an incredible Welsh sportsman. In addition to devising these rules, he also staged an FA cup final and the Thames Regatta, instituted championships for billiards, cycling and athletics, rowed across the English Channel and edited a national newspaper. Although he wrote the rules, they were published under Queensberry's sponsorship and hence were publicized under that name. In which sport would you follow these rules?

4. This was one of the first sports to be played in the Olympics, having been part of the programme since 1896. There are three forms of this sport, which are classified according to the kind of weapon they use. Consequently, the rules are different for each as well. This activity shifted from military training to sport thanks to Domenico Angelo, who established an academy for the same in 1763. He established the rules of posture and footwork that still govern the modern

form of the sport. Which sport is this that is divided into foil, épée and sabre?

5. This is a type of combat sport which originated in Thailand and became widespread in the last century. It is referred to as the 'art of eight limbs', as an athlete has the combined use of fists, elbows, knees and shins, thus using eight points of contact. Legend has it that a famous fighter called Nai Khanomtom was captured in the year 1767 and he managed to knock out ten consecutive Burmese contenders. As a reward, he was granted freedom and returned to Siam (present day Thailand) where he was heralded as a hero and his fighting style became famous. What sport is this, whose name literally means 'combat from Thailand'?

6. Ann Maria De Mars was the first American to win a gold medal at the World Judo Championships in 1984. She pursued a PhD in educational psychology and went on to become the Chief Executive Officer of 7 Generation Games, and also authored grants for various Native American programmes. She was named in the Forbes '40 Women to Watch Over 40 list in 2013. She trained her youngest daughter who, at the age of seventeen, qualified to become the youngest judoka at the 2004 Athens Olympics. Four years later, at the 2008 Beijing Olympics, she won a bronze medal, becoming the first ever American to win an Olympic medal in women's judo. She went on to have a stellar career in mixed martial arts and became the first female fighter to be inducted into the UFC Hall of Fame. Who is this

daughter who is currently taking part in the WWE and has appeared in a Fast and Furious film?

7. This is a type of Korean martial art that emphasizes head-height kicks, jumping and spinning kicks, and fast kicking techniques. It was developed in the late 1940s as a mix of Chinese martial arts and indigenous Korean martial arts traditions such as Taekkyeon, Subak and Gwonbeop. It became an Olympic sport at the 2000 Sydney Olympics and in 2012 became a Commonwealth Games sport. The name of the sport comes from three Korean words which together mean 'the way of the foot and fist'. What is the name of this martial sport form?

8. This is a Japanese martial art which deals with close combat where one learns that the most efficient methods for neutralizing an opponent is through pins, joint locks and throws. The athlete is taught to use an opponent's energy against him, rather than directly opposing it. The two-word name can be translated as meaning 'gentle technique'. There is a version which has been recognized as an official sport of the World Games, where there are three categories: self-defense demonstration, freefighting and grappling. What sport is this that expresses the philosophy of yielding to an opponent's force, rather than trying to oppose it?

9. Buhurt is a modern full-contact fighting sport in which the combatants have to use armour and weapons in the style of those made between 1200 and 1699 CE. An athlete's full set of armour must originate from

the same place and from within a fifty-year time span. Unlike staged battles one would see at historical re-enactments, these are actual combats which have referees. Some of the categories one can participate in are 'shield-sword', 'sword-sword' and longsword. The name 'buhurt' comes from the old French word béhourd which means 'wallop'. The more common usage for this event is HMB which is an abbreviation of what this event is. What is the full form of HMB?

10. Savate is a combat sport that uses the hands and feet as weapons, combining elements of English boxing with graceful kicking techniques. The name comes from the word for 'old shoe' from the language of the country of origin. This refers to the heavy footwear which the military used to wear. The combat techniques evolved from the type of street fighting which was common at the beginning of the nineteenth century in the capital city of this country. A possible explanation for this style of fighting is that it was developed in this way to allow the fighter to use a hand to hold onto something for balance on a rocking ship's deck, and that the kicks and slaps were used on land to avoid the legal penalties for using a closed fist, which was considered a deadly weapon under the law. The common name for this sport is a direct reference to the country of origin of this sport. What is savate better known as?

ANSWERS

1. Judo
2. Sparta
3. Boxing
4. Fencing
5. Muay Thai
6. Ronda Rousey
7. Taekwondo
8. Jujutsu
9. Historical Medieval Battles
10. French boxing

9. OTHER SPORTS

1. Sports such as football and basketball have sent countless students to college. Robert Morris University in Chicago is taking things in a different direction. They allow their applicants to earn athletic scholarships from their couches. They offer students the chance to compete for scholarships by playing a game that was launched in 2009 and currently has over 100 million active players each month. What game do these students play, whose name gets abbreviated to LoL?

2. This is a game played with a flying disc, some wickets and empty cups. It is usually played with teams of two. The wickets are placed in the form of a rectangle with the poles about 15in. apart and the next pair of poles is planted in the same way 40ft away. The cups are kept on top of the wickets and the opponent tries to throw the disc between the other team's wickets without knocking off the cups. If the knocked-off cup is caught by a receiving team member with one hand

before it touches the ground, the receiving team earns 1 point, and if the disc passes between the wickets the throwing team earns 2 points. The name of the sport is a portmanteau of the names of the most popular flying disc and the most popular game which has wickets. What is the name of this sport?

3. This game, though in existence since ancient Roman times, was first mentioned in the 1672 *Book of Games* where the author describes it as a 'play with a piece of tile...play upon any area divided into oblong figures like boards'. In Puerto Rico, these playing areas are supposed to refer to the nine circles a stranger has to pass through to enter heaven as in the *Divine Comedy* by Dante. This game is known by different names such as escargot, peevers, pabats, nondi etc. How do we better know this game that you would have probably encountered for the first time in school?

4. Vatimanjuvirattu, velivirattu and vatammanjuvirattu are variants of this sport. It is based on the concept of 'flight or flight', where multiple participants take part at the same time and are judged on the amount of time they are able to hang on to the object that has been released. This sport is traditionally held during the harvest festival in Tamil Nadu. What sport is this that has been at the centre of much controversy over the past few years?

5. In the early days, balls for this sport were made using the inflated bladders of a certain animal and so they took on a particular shape. They were much larger and

rounder than the balls used today. The peculiar shape also made it convenient for the players to carry them, as the game involved more running with the balls than kicking them. The green-coloured bladders had to be inflated using the stem of a clay pipe before being encased in leather and hand-stitched. Only in 1870 was the inflatable rubber bladder invented, but the basic stitching techniques are pretty much the same from the earlier days. What game is this and which animal's bladder was initially used as a ball?

6. Juego del pato is the national sport of Argentina and is a combination of polo and basketball. Players on horseback compete to fight for possession of a ball that has six handles, and score by throwing it through a vertically positioned ring. The sport, also known as Pato, was banned several times because of the violence that was part of it. Many riders were trampled underfoot and many more lost their lives to knife fights that happened during the game. The name Pato comes from the Spanish word for a type of bird that was used instead of the ball in the early days. What is the bird that 'Pato' refers to, one that you would have most probably heard in of in cricket?

7. The Chinnaswamy Stadium in Bangalore has a brick wall at its entrance that is 27ft high, 15ft wide and is made of 10,000 bricks. This was erected in 2008. A live electronic counter on one corner of the wall ticked from then on, until it finally stopped in 2012, at the number 13288. Emblazoned with the words

'commitment, consistency, class', this structure has been erected to honour which great sportsperson (who was still playing when it was built)?

8. These games were first described by the historian Pausanias in 175 CE. He described a ritual that took place in ancient Greece, where unmarried women took part in athletic events (foot races) on a competitive basis. These games are assumed to have been started because women were banned from the Olympic Games (only unmarried women could even be spectators!). They also took place every four years and the women's foot races took place in the same stadium, but with a shorter course. There are very few descriptions of these games and none before Pausanias. We also do not know how old these games were. Some scholars speculate that they could be almost as old as the Olympic Games. While the Olympic Games were dedicated to Zeus, the Lord of Olympus, after whom was the female equivalent of the games named?

9. The earliest record of this sport is from the sixteenth century in Scotland. The oldest club of this sport was started in Scotland in 1716 and is still in operation today. The game is said to have originated when players used flat-bottomed stones from rivers or fields and played on frozen rivers. Initially it was more a game of luck, whereas the professional version of the sport practised today requires precision, skill and strategy. The sport has been included in the Winter Olympics since 1998. The stone that is used is made of granite

which comes from either one of two sources, an island off Scotland or a quarry in Wales. This sport has an unusual player called a sweeper, who uses a broom to sweep the path of the stone if required, to change the distance or direction. What is the name of this sport, which comes from the name of the curved path the stone takes as it slides?

10. The Axel jump is named after Norwegian Axel Paulsen who, in 1882, became the first person in the sport to perform this jump. The triple Axel jump is considered to be the most technically difficult jump and has the highest base value of 8.0. Only nine female athletes have landed this jump in international competitions. Rena Inoue and John Baldwin, Jr. of the US became the first pair to perform a triple Axel in competition in 2006 and repeated the feat at the 2006 Winter Olympics. In which sport does the Axel jump feature?

11. Alfréd Hajós was a Hungarian athlete who was dubbed the 'Hungarian dolphin' by Greek newspapers in 1896. He is the first Olympic gold medallist (in modern Olympics) in a certain discipline and went on to win another gold medal at the same Olympics in the same field (one in the 100m and one in the 1200m). After the 1896 Olympics, Alfréd Hajôs returned to Hungary and went on to become an architect. In 1924, he returned to the Olympics to win yet another medal, and although he won a silver medal, there was no gold awarded, and for all practical purposes he had won the top medal. The category in which he won

the medal was only included between 1912 and 1948. Baron Pierre de Coubertin, the founder of the modern Olympic Games, had fought hard for this category to be included, stating that it was given equal importance in the Olympic Games of Ancient Greece. What was Alfréd Hajós' third Olympic medal for?

12. This athlete has set speed records and then broken them himself! At the 2008 Olympics, he became the first man to set world records in three events, the 100m, 200m and 4x100m relay, at the same Olympics. He is also the first man to have won two gold medals in the same two events for three consecutive Olympics (the 100m and 200m events). As of 2019, he holds the world record of 9.58sec. for the 100m, a speed reflected in the title of his memoir *My Story: 9.58 – The World's Fastest Man*. Who is this incredible athlete who first excelled as a fast bowler and loved football, before being redirected to his field by a perceptive coach?

13. In August 2018, Tata Power claimed that they had set up the world's largest rooftop installation of a certain kind at a cricket stadium at the Cricket Club of India in Mumbai. The project, completed in a hundred days, is projected to save the club 25 per cent of its current expenditure and curb over 840 tons of CO_2 emissions. What is this interesting installation?

14. During the First World War, there was a huge rise in the visibility and popularity of women's football in the UK. A group of women in a munitions factory, who used to play during the break, were spotted by an office

administrator, Alfred Frankland, who realized that they could be successful, and proposed that they set up a team. This team went to become a phenomenal success. They played what is possibly the first ladies' international in this field and packed 53,000 spectators into a field (with an estimated 14,000 stuck outside, unable to get in). Their most successful player was Lily Parr, who scored 43 goals in one season and 1000 goals overall in her career (including one that broke a male goalkeeper's arm because he was convinced she couldn't get a penalty kick by him). In 1921, alarmed that the men's sport could be losing out, the official governing body banned all affiliated grounds from hosting women's matches, effectively banning the sport for women. This ban was only overturned in the UK in 1971. The team then chose to tour, and played in the US, playing the men's teams (no women's team for the sport existed yet in the US) and won 6 out of 9 matches! What was the name of this legendary, path-breaking team that broke all barriers?

15. This team won six consecutive Olympic golds in their event, a feat unparalleled thus far. Further, at the 1956 Olympics, they set the record of winning their gold medal without having conceded a single goal across all five matches, while scoring 38 goals themselves. What incredible team was this and what was the sport they dominated across decades?

ANSWERS

1. League of Legends
2. Fricket (Frisbee + cricket)
3. Hopskotch
4. Jallikattu
5. Rugby, pig's bladders
6. Duck
7. Rahul Dravid
8. Hera, they were called the Heraia or Heraean Games
9. Curling
10. Figure-skating
11. The Olympics Arts Competition, for a stadium design he submitted
12. Usain Bolt
13. Roof-mounted solar power plant
14. The Dick, Kerr Ladies F.C.
15. The Indian field hockey team

10. FIRSTS AND LASTS

1. At the 1988 Seoul Olympic Games, in a certain equestrian event called dressage, which has a unique feature of participation, the following were the winners: Nicole Uphoff from Germany (gold), Margit Otto-Crépin from France (silver) and Christine Stückelberger from Switzerland (bronze). The event had been introduced in 1912, but only in 1952 was a pioneering change made to the rule based on the fact that the attributes required to be successful are to be a confident and able rider of horses, which anyone can do. This change led to this path-breaking result. What was this result and what is special about this event?

2. This athlete was the first to clear 6.1m in his sport. He set 35 world records, breaking his own record 14 times. He won the IAAF World Championships 6 times, setting a record. He was also, interestingly, among the first delegates representing his country at the Summer Olympics in 1996. However, his only

Olympic gold medal was won for another country at the 1988 Olympics. Who is this legendary athlete and what was the sport in which he constantly reached new heights?

3. The first edition of this now-iconic annual sporting event took place in 1829. The winner of the inaugural race was the older of the two participating bodies. Although the event is known by the name of the two participating teams, it takes place on a water body in a third city (one city in 1829 and another in the next edition, where it has remained till date). What is the event and which are the two participating bodies?

4. 1877, 1881, 1891, 1905: all four years represent the first edition of events that now take place on an annual basis and are collectively known by a two-word term. Strictly speaking, this term is used only in the case where all four events are won in the same year. The first person to achieve this was Don Budge in 1938. What sport and what events are these?

5. In 2004, this player became the first cricketer to score 400 runs in a Test match, achieving this feat against England. In 1994 he also became the first batsman to score 500 runs in a match in first class cricket (a record unbeaten as of July 2019). Who is this swashbuckling batsman who retired in 2007?

6. In January 2018, Leicester City scored a goal to go up 2-0 against Fleetwood. The Leicester City striker had scored but he was initially ruled to be offside (which meant the goal was not counted). An assistant referee

then clarified that he was not offside and awarded him the goal. What was unique about this decision in English football?

7. The 2019 edition of the Wimbledon Tennis Championships will be the first edition played with a certain new rule in place. This rule was brought in following two record-length matches (both, interestingly, featuring John Isner). After loud demands from the tennis world, the Championship agreed to compromise with this proud tradition and brought in a halfway measure. What is this new rule?

8. While a student at Oxford, this future neurologist became the first person to run a mile in under 4 minutes. While his feat itself was remarkable, it was seen as even more remarkable because he had to overcome the widely-held belief that this was an impossible task. He is believed to have used his medical training to scientifically train himself. He graduated from Oxford the same year (1954) as the one in which he achieved his feat. His record was broken by a certain John Landy. He then raced Landy later in 1954 and both men finished the race in under 4 minutes, which was another first in the athletic world. The Oxford graduate won that race and then retired to devote himself to his medical career. Who was this athletic neurologist who went on to be knighted?

9. In 1998, when France lifted the football World Cup, Lucien Laurent was the only surviving member of the 1930 World Cup squad to watch this feat. The 1930

squad had played in the first ever FIFA World Cup, in Uruguay. It seems fitting that Laurent was able to watch his team lift the trophy given that he holds an important first in the world of football. What is this first?

10. Zahra Nemati, a black belt in taekwondo, was in a car accident that left her with both legs paralysed. She took up archery, and in just 6 months finished third in the National Championships, where she was competing against professional archers. She became her nation's first-ever female athlete to earn an Olympic or Paralympic title when she won an individual gold in women's archery and a team bronze at the 2012 Summer Paralympics in London. She went on to be only the third female flag bearer for her country during the opening ceremony of the 2016 Rio Olympics. Which country does she represent?

11. In 1956, this sportsperson became the first black tennis player to win a Grand Slam tournament at the French Open. This player then went on to become the first black tennis player to win Wimbledon and the US Open (1957 and 1958, respectively). In order to fund their career, this player toured with the Harlem Globetrotters, playing tennis before the team came on to play basketball. Who is this fantastic tennis player who also went on to play golf (albeit, not with as much success)?

12. Pál Szekeres is a Hungarian fencer who won a bronze medal in the team foil event at the 1988 Seoul Summer

Olympics. In 1991, he was injured in a bus accident. The very next year he took part in the 1992 Paralympics in Barcelona and won a gold medal in foil, going on to win two more golds at the 1996 Paralympics in Atlanta. What unique first (and only one as of 2019) does Szekeres have to his name?

13. On 18 July 1976, this Romanian gymnast finished her routine on the uneven bars and waited for the judges to score her performance. The audience and her coach were expecting a high score as she had done an outstanding routine. So, when the electronic scoreboard showed a score of 1.0, the crowd and the athlete were aghast. However, when the reason behind this display was explained, it delighted the coach and the athlete and made news all around the world. Who was this athlete and what was this the first instance of at the Olympics?

14. At the 1968 Mexico Summer Olympics, African-American sprinter Jim Hines won the 100m final. The light beam reading at the finish line showed his time to be 9.89sec. but was later followed by the official Polaroid film-based timing of 9.95sec. Later in the day his team went on to win the 4x100m in which he ran his 100m in just 8.2sec. What significant 'first' did Jim Hines achieve in the field of athletics?

15. Captain Matthew Webb was an employee of Kellog's. In 1875, he was the first to achieve a certain feat for sport and without any artificial aid. He achieved this in less than 22 hours and became a hugely popular

figure. Since his achievement, so many people have emulated this feat that there is now an association for this purpose and bookings have to be made two years in advance, in addition to other training and approvals. What was Captain Webb the first person to do?

ANSWERS

1. Dressage is unique in that it is an Olympic event where both men and women participate at the same time and against each other (inter-sex event). At this event for the first time all three winners were women.

2. Sergey Bubka (Ukraine), pole vaulting

3. The Thames River Boat Race, Oxford and Cambridge Universities

4. Tennis, the Grand Slam tournaments (Wimbledon, US Open, French Open and Australian Open)

5. Brian Lara, West Indies

6. The first goal awarded by VAR: Video Assistant Referee

7. A tie-breaker in the fifth set at 12–12

8. Sir Roger Bannister

9. First World Cup goal scored

10. Iran

11. Althea Gibson; she was the first black golfer to join the LPGA

12. First person to have won medals at both the Olympic and Paralympic Games

13. Nadia Comaneci, she got a perfect score of 10 but the display had not been calibrated to display a perfect score as it was thought to be impossible
14. First person to break the 10-second barrier
15. Swim across the English Channel

11. PEOPLE IN SPORTS

1. This sportsman-turned-sports bureaucrat was robbed of his £11,000 Hublot watch and was hit hard in the face outside his office. Before the stitches were removed, he contacted Hublot, who was the official timekeeper for the sport he governs, and created an ad which had a picture of his disfigured face and said, 'See what people would do for a Hublot'. Who was this enterprising person and which multi-billion dollar sport did he oversee for three decades?

2. Fanny Blankers-Koen, who was dubbed 'the flying housewife', finished the 1948 London Olympic Games with four gold medals. She was knighted by the Queen of Netherlands and was given a gift from the city of Amsterdam. While being given the gift, she was told this was to help her 'go through life at a slower pace' and 'so she need not run so much'. What fitting gift was given by the city of Amsterdam to Fanny Blankers-Koen?

3. This person pioneered the concept of a tennis boarding school. Some of the top tennis players his school has produced are Andre Agassi, Jim Courier, Monica Seles and Mary Pierce. He served as a First Lieutenant in the US Army and then dropped out of a law course to start a tennis camp that changed the way tennis was taught at the elite junior level. Currently owned by International Management Group, the academy still has him playing a pivotal role in its programmes. Who is this person who wrote an autobiography titled *My Aces, My Faults*?

4. Joe DiMaggio, Sugar Ray Robinson, Rocky Marciano, Roy Campanella, Brooklyn Dodgers, Mickey Mantle, Sonny Liston and Floyd Patterson. These legendary sportspeople and teams are in an exhaustive list which is of a chronological nature. Where would you find these entities?

5. Nineteen-year-old Yoshinori Sakai was the final torch runner and the one chosen to light the Olympic Flame at the 1964 Tokyo Games. Although he never took part in the Games, he did win a gold in the 1600m relay and a silver in the 400m at the Bangkok Asian Games. In 2014, he passed away due to a cerebral haemorrhage. For what specific and sentimental reason was Sakai chosen to light the Olympic Flame in Japan?

6. The story goes that Richard Klein was brainstorming for a new name for his franchise. He wanted to use either Matador or Toreador as a name for his team. When he discussed the idea with his sons, one of

them thought it was a terrible choice and used a fitting phrase to reply. Klein thought it was serendipitous and used that exclamation as the name of the team. Which team, that once ruled the arena in the mid 90s, thus got its name?

7. It all started for this young man in 2008 with Julie, followed by Kate, Abbey, Hungry Heidi, Suzie, Eva, Magherita, Gina, Loria and the latest being Lina. Lina is officially known as SF90. What are these and who is the young man who over the past eleven years has broken many records and won four World Championships?

8. This gentleman was a French tennis player who was one among four athletes who dominated the game in the 1920s and 30s. He was world number one in 1926 and 1927 and was part of the team that won the Davis Cup in 1927 and 1928. He was nicknamed 'the crocodile' and there are multiple theories as to why. One says that it refers to his tenacity while playing. His son provided a theory where apparently the player had seen a suitcase made of crocodile skin in a shop, which was also the reward for a bet. Consequently, his friend embroidered a crocodile onto the blazer that he wore. In 1933, he founded a company in his name that produced a tennis shirt which had an iconic logo that referred to his nickname. What was this sportsman's name?

9. Richard Raskind was an ophthalmologist who captained the Yale tennis team and won a New

York state title. In the 1960 US National Tennis Championships (later to be known as the US Open), Richard faced and lost to Neale Fraser who went on to become the champion. After a period of hibernation, the player came back to the same tournament in 1987 but ended up losing to Virginia Wade in the first round and reached the final in the doubles. What is unique about this achievement?

10. Gordon Smith, Bobby Johnstone, Lawrie Reilly, Eddie Turnbull and Willie Ormond of the Hibernian Football Club were all part of the three-time League Championship winning team. They helped the team reach the semi-finals of the European Cup. By what name were they known? It should remind you of a popular children's series by Enid Blyton?

11. At the 1968 Mexico Olympics, this person was the clear favourite to win the gold medal in his event. What was unexpected was the way he was going to go about it. He made his run up and executed his very first try on the field. After about 15 minutes of the judges having to use their tape measure, the announcer called out the distance. The athlete, not familiar with metric measurements, was not aware of what he had just done, but his coach came up to him and told him that he had broken the world record by an incredible margin of 55cm. The world record which had been changing almost every year till then, became one that stood for twenty-three years. Who was this athlete and in which event was this iconic record set?

12. This British-South African environmentalist uses incredible swims to highlight ecological damage across the world. He is the first person to have completed long-distance swims in every ocean in the world and in 2018 he became the first person to swim the length of the English Channel, starting at Cornwall and ending at Dover, describing the plastic pollution he saw along the way. He is also the first person to swim across one of the 'ends of the world', to highlight the effects of global warming. Where was this and who is this magnificent swimmer?

13. This Czechoslovak long-distance runner started working at a Bata shoe factory at the age of sixteen. The factory sports coach ordered him to run, and though he protested, he ended up second. Just six years later, he was selected for the national team. His greatest feat was recorded at the 1952 Summer Olympics at Helsinki. He ran and won the 5000m and the 10000m and broke the world records in both. After this, at the last minute, he decided to compete in the marathon, an event he had never participated in before. He raced alongside the then record-holder Jim Peters for 15km and then just accelerated, winning the gold and setting another world record in the process. He remains the only person to have won all three long-distance events in the same Olympic Games. Who was this legendary person who was known as the 'Czech locomotive' because of the way he ran?

14. This athlete is said to be the greatest in his sport and

is ranked the 'greatest North American sportsperson of the twentieth century'. His leaping ability earned him the nickname 'His Airness'. Nike exclusively produced a range of shoes for him which was eventually made accessible to the public. He is the very first athlete to have become a billionaire. Who is this person who led his team to seven titles and his country to two Olympic golds?

15. This sportsperson, at the age of twenty, became the youngest heavyweight champion in the history of his sport. At one point of time, he held the three most important titles at the same time. At the Junior Olympics, he once won a match with a knockout in eight seconds flat. His most infamous moment arrived when he got tired of his opponent, headbutting him and biting off a piece of his ear. He became popular again with his cameos in a series of films about a gang of friends who end up in disastrous situations after partying. Who is this champion with a wild streak?

ANSWERS

1. Bernie Ecclestone
2. A cycle
3. Nick Bollettieri
4. The song 'We didn't start the fire' by Billy Joel
5. He was born in Hiroshima on 6 August 1945, an hour and a half after the atomic bomb was dropped.

6. Chicago Bulls

7. Sebastian Vettel's F1 cars

8. René Lacoste

9. First transgender person to play professional tennis

10. The Famous Five

11. Bob Beamon, long jump

12. North Pole, Lewis Pugh

13. Emil Zátopek

14. Michael Jordan

15. Mike Tyson

12. ARENAS AND STADIA

1. This stadium was the largest in the country when it was rebuilt in 2007. The new structure replaced a stadium that had existed since the 1920s and which hosted the 1948 Olympics and a historic home win in the 1966 FIFA World Cup finals. The most striking feature of this stadium is a giant arch that contributes to roof support and ensures that every seat in the stadium has an unimpeded view of proceedings. The arch is so tall that it had to have a beacon to warn low-flying planes!

   In addition to sports, it's also a world-famous performance venue. In addition to all this, it has the undeniably major attraction of 2,618 toilets, which is reportedly the largest number of toilet facilities in any stadium in the world. A definite winning situation, as fans would no doubt agree. What impressive stadium is this that is jokingly referred to as the 'picnic basket'?

2. When it was built in 1984, this stadium was the

largest stadium in the world dedicated to football, and the second-largest stadium in the world, across all sports. As of 2019, it remains India's largest stadium by capacity and is the home of the Indian national football team. Situated in Bidhannagar, the name of the stadium comes from what the place was earlier known as. Officially known as Vivekananda Yuba Bharati Krirangan (VYBK), it's popular name comes from the fact that the whole area of the township used to be a huge salty marsh studded with little fishing villages along its edges. What spectacular stadium is this, located in a state that may rightfully be called India's most passionate football state?

3. This stadium has witnessed two key moments in its nation's history, in addition to many international sporting triumphs. It was the site of the first speech made in his home city by a political leader who had just been released from prison after twenty-seven years of incarceration. It was also, sadly, the site of his last public appearance (in 2010). In 2013, his memorial service was also held here. In addition to its close association with this leader, the stadium has also served as the venue for the 2010 opening and closing ceremonies of the FIFA World Cup as well as for the final match of that World Cup. It is the largest stadium on its continent and has hosted many other international sporting events as well as big-name concerts. Earlier christened Soccer City, it was rebuilt for the 2010 FIFA World Cup and was nicknamed the 'Calabash', because its colours and shape resembled

that of the 'calabash' or cooking pot kept on a flame. How is this famous stadium known today and who is the global figure who made his presence felt on its grounds?

4. The Borg El Arab stadium is the second-largest stadium in the African continent. It has the distinction of being entirely constructed by the _____ Armed Forces Corps of Engineers. Despite its size, the stadium has not, unfortunately, been able to host many major matches and also faces competition from several other famous stadia in the country. In what country is this stadium located, historically known for many, many other famous constructions?

5. This arena, located in Michigan in the US, was home to the NHL hockey team that has won the most number of Stanley Cup championships in the US (11). However, the last hockey game played here was in 2017 and the arena began to be demolished in 2019. Over the years, it has hosted various NHL games, NBA games, soccer games as well as concerts and (in 1980) the Republican National Convention in which Ronald Reagan was nominated as a presidential candidate. Its last event was a WWE match featuring John Cena. The arena itself, though associated with hockey and historical scores in basketball, was named after a legendary American boxer from the city, known as the Brown Bomber. What is the name of this historical arena?

6. This sporting venue hosted the first Test match between

two iconic cricketing countries. Established in 1853, it predates several major historical events, including the Eiffel Tower, India's First War of Independence and the American Civil War. It is the largest sporting venue on its continent and has hosted an Olympic Games, an edition of the Commonwealth Games as well as other sports such as football, rugby and track bicycle racing! During the Second Word War, it housed the country's Royal Air Force. It has hosted multiple concerts and cultural events. It is best-known for being the regular venue of a sporting event that takes place on the day after Christmas every year, with any opponents who are part of the summer tour in the country. What iconic venue is this, with world-famous light towers?

7. The largest stadium in the world is located in the capital city of a certain country and, while playing host to a variety of sporting events, this venue currently has the highest attendance during the Mass Games conducted in that country. During this, performances take place in the centre of the venue, while spectators hold up coloured panels or paper so that together, when viewed from above, the stands form a colourful mural depicting scenes that reflect the theme of the performance. The size of this stadium may seem intriguing to international audiences, given the historical isolationism of this country. In which country is the May Day Stadium located?

8. The Kingsmead Cricket Ground in Durban used to host the Boxing Day Test match when a test was played

in South Africa. It also hosted 15 matches of the 2009 IPL series when it was moved out of India due to the general elections. It is also the ground in which Yuvraj Singh smashed six consecutive sixes off Stuart Broad in 2007. The stadium has a famous myth doing the rounds, that a certain natural phenomenon affects the batting conditions as it is built quite close to the beach. What phenomenon is supposed to affect the batting in this stadium?

9. This famous baseball stadium in Houston was dubbed the 'eighth wonder of the world' when it was built, and was the first stadium in the world with a domed roof. It was the home ground of the Houston baseball team as well as two NFL teams. Although it was officially named the Harris County Domed Stadium, it became famous under its present name, right from its opening in 1965, when it hosted an exhibition match between the New York Yankees and the Houston _____ (who were known earlier as the Houston Colts .45). The name given to the stadium, as well as the Houston team's new name, was a tribute to another famous institution also located in Houston. The stadium also hosted several cultural performances, the first entertainer to perform here being Judy Garland. It went on to feature Elvis Presley, The Rolling Stones and also a Muhammad Ali fight. By what name did the world know this stadium, which was completely stripped in 2016 and earmarked for redevelopment by 2020, after being identified as a firetrap?

10. This structure, famous under another name, is also known as the Flavian Amphitheater, since it was built during the reign of the Flavian empires, and is indisputably one of the most famous in the world. It was an architectural marvel in its day for its freestanding structure and also had retractable awnings to offer shade to the 50,000 spectators it could hold! Although this venue deteriorated in the medieval times, it is still standing and can be visited. It is estimated that in the contests that took place here while it was an active venue, over a million animals and 5,00,000 human beings died. What is the name by which most people know this structure with a gruesome history of entertainment, and where is it found?

11. This is one of the few instances in sports where an entire town is the venue for a sporting event. The sport uses public roads in the town for its path, although certain modifications and restrictions have been brought in over the years for the safety of the public as well as the participants. It has played host to some of the biggest manufacturers of the equipment used in the sport and is the world's oldest endurance racing form in its sport. What is this annual event that covers an entire day around a single path in a town in Europe?

12. The Dubai International Cricket Stadium is part of the Dubai Sports City. It is lit by a special system of 350 floodlights that are fixed around the circumference of its round roof, thereby minimizing the shadows of objects on the ground and having no light towers.

What is the name given to this lighting system that sounds like something from a J.R.R. Tolkien novel?

13. This multi-purpose arena hosts ice hockey, basketball, boxing and wrestling matches as well as huge concerts and circuses. It opened in 1968 and at that time was one of the most expensive stadiums in the world. It is named after the fourth president of the US and it used to host P.T. Barnum's circuses. A brilliant feature of this arena is that the ice rests underneath the basketball court with a layer of insulated material between them. This allows the arena to host ice hockey and basketball matches on the same day. It also has a unique concave ceiling as opposed to the usual convex one which gives it an excellent acoustic quality, making it a concert Mecca. What is the name of this iconic arena which refers to the place it is in and not its shape?

14. This purpose-built, banked oval racing circuit is nicknamed 'The Brickyard' and was the first to be called a 'Speedway'. With a capacity of 2,57,325 it is the highest-capacity sports venue in the world. It is the only national historic landmark affiliated to automotive racing history. Named after the city it is found in, the stadium used to host the US Grand Prix in Formula One. What is the name of this Speedway?

15. This cricket ground was named after its founder and is home to the world's oldest sporting museum. It is known for its mix of old and new architecture, from the pavilion which has remained the same since the Victorian era to the futuristic-looking media centre which was the first

all-aluminium, semi-monocoque building in the world. Amongst the usual cricket matches, the stadium has also hosted the first ever major one-day tournament in 1963, a baseball match during World War I and also the archery event during the 2012 Summer Olympics. Which iconic ground is this?

ANSWERS

1. Wembley Stadium

2. Salt Lake Stadium, Kolkata

3. First National Bank (FNB) Stadium, Nelson Mandela

4. Egypt

5. Joe Louis Arena, Detroit

6. Melbourne Cricket Ground, Australia

7. Pyongyang, North Korea

8. The rise and fall of the tide

9. Astrodome ('Astro' after the NASA Space Centre in Houston)

10. The Colosseum, Rome

11. Le 24 heures du Mans (the 24 hours of Le Mans, endurance motor sport racing)

12. The Ring of Fire

13. Madison Square Garden

14. Indianapolis Motor Speedway

15. Lord's Cricket Ground

13. SPORTING TERMS

1. One explanation for the origin of this term is that baseball fields were earlier oriented to be in a westerly direction when facing the batter. Thus, the pitcher's left hand would be towards the south. However, this origin is often disputed, given that this term did not originate with baseball at all (and not all baseball fields are oriented in this manner) and was used much earlier to describe a left-handed person dealing a blow. What term is this?

2. This term is associated with golf, tennis and baseball (though with varying uses). However, its origins can actually be traced back to a card game, as far back as 1800 CE, where it described winning all thirteen tricks in a game of bridge. What interesting term is this?

3. In business-to-business dealings, it's quite common for one company to be lagging behind in the decision-making process. When everything has been done on

one end to make a decision and they are waiting for the other side to make a decision, a certain phrase is used. This phrase stems from a stalling tactic in both tennis and basketball which means it's up to the opponent to take the next step. What is the phrase?

4. This term is used in chess to refer to a situation in which a player does not have any more legal moves to play, despite their king not facing a check. In other situations, it is also used to refer to any situation or event where two parties are stuck in a deadlock and neither can advance. What is this term that signals an impasse?

5. An explanation for this cricketing term states that it comes from the fact that the delivery used would cause a batsman's eyes to goggle or would shock him. What is the term that we now use, based on this, for a tricky delivery in cricket, or any situation in real life that throws up an unexpected twist?

6. This term comes from the French word for 'youngest' and is also where we get the term 'cadet' from. In this sport, it refers to an assistant who carries the player's equipment and offers moral support and advice. What is this friendly assistant called and in which sport is the term used?

7. This term seems to arise from the fact that when a bowler takes a certain number of wickets, their club shows their appreciation by gifting them with a piece of headgear. What is this term that is now used across sports (and even outside sports) to refer to someone

achieving something in a specific number?

8. This entity is made of vulcanized rubber and serves the same function as a ball. The sport it is most associated with is known for its speed and its frequent physical contact. The game is an Olympic sport and very popular in the North American continent. Initially, the item was square in shape and made of wood. The first rubber versions were made by slicing a rubber ball and trimming the disc to make it square. Eventually, in 1880, the Victoria Hockey Club started making round ones which became the norm. Colloquially it is also known as a 'biscuit' because of its shape, which leads to the expression 'put the biscuit in the basket' which means to score a goal. In which sport is this used and what is the name of this entity which sounds like a character from a William Shakespeare play?

9. This expression for winning convincingly comes from the sport of horse-racing. It originally referred to a jockey who is so far ahead that he can afford to slacken off and still win a race without whipping his horse or pulling back the reins. What is this expression that commentators use quite often?

10. This collection of terms all refer to a score of 0 in this particular sport. The basic version is the name of a water fowl, referring to a person who has not managed to score any runs at all. If the person manages to be dismissed on the first ball then the bird is preceded by a precious metal. If somehow the person is dismissed without facing a delivery (run out etc.) then the bird

is preceded by a gem. What are these three terms and in which sport would you see them being used?

11. In rowing, after you remove your oar from the water, you flip it so that it is parallel to the water as you prepare for another stroke. If you fail to remove the oar on time, the blade acts like a brake, and the handle whips back towards you. This is called 'catching a ____,' which refers to a certain crustacean who might hurt you if you handle it the wrong way. What is the term which rowers hope they don't have to use?

12. In the late nineteenth century, America used to export nutmegs to England. Sometimes, sellers would place wooden nuts in the sacks along with real nutmegs, tricking the buyers into paying extra for essentially nothing. Nutmeging subsequently started referring to a smart move on the side of the seller and stupidity on the side of the buyer. This term is used in a particular sport where a player can 'nutmeg' an opponent by kicking the ball between their legs, then sprint around the defender and regain possession of it. It is an effective move both tactically and emotionally: nutmeging your opponent can give you a serious mental edge. In which sport would you see this move which has been perfected by one certain Luis Suarez?

13. A deke is a fake-out in ice hockey, in which the puckhandler uses quick, controlled movements with the puck to get around his defender. The term comes from the shortening of a particular word by Canadians. The verb form of this word means 'to lure or entice

away from intended course'. 'Deke' is the Canadian version of which word?

14. Pepper is a warm-up routine among exponents of a particular sport. It usually consists of two athletes separated by 5–20ft performing the following sequence of movements: bump, set, spike, repeat. Player 1 then passes the ball back to player 2, starting the drill. Player 2 sets the ball back to player 1. Player 1 spikes the ball back, forcing player 2 to dig the ball where player 1 can set it, allowing player 2 to spike it. Player 1 passes the spiked ball, and the cycle starts all over again. Which sport would you be getting ready to play if you were peppering?

15. This term, which comes from a certain sport, has become part of the English language now and means a 'forceful, dramatic move, especially against someone'. In the sport, it refers to a forceful shot in which the player jumps right into the scoring area and forces the ball in. It has become such an integral and entertaining part of the sport that separate competitions are held only for this move. What is this move?

16. Bookmakers at racing matches used to put up bets on a sign or a board. A person could bet on a horse to come first, second or third. If someone bet equal amounts on all three, a certain term was used to indicate that they were making an appearance all over the sign where the bets were noted, and this term has now entered common parlance to mean something that is comprehensive or wide-ranging. What is this

interesting term?

17. In boxing, if an opponent is knocked out (flat on the ground) and does not get up before the referee counts to ten, they are said to be 'out' and they lose the match. Each bout or contest in boxing is made up of multiple rounds of fixed time and the opponent may be lucky if the round ends before the count to 10 is completed. This is thought to have given rise to a term that is commonly used to talk about someone who escapes something at the last minute. What is this interesting four-word term?

18. In American football, this term is used to describe a desperate situation where a player needs to get their ball to the other end of the field and throws it as far as they can, hoping that someone can intercept it and make the touchdown (carrying the ball across the opposing team's goal-line). In 1975, Roger Staubach, a Dallas Cowboys player, made a last-minute touchdown in this way and described it as closing your eyes, saying a prayer and throwing it. What specific prayer did he mention, which is now associated with all such moves?

19. Yet another term that comes from boxing, this one refers to the fact that a boxer almost always has a second or support staff in their part of the ring who provides physical and moral support between rounds. The phrase is now used to indicate that you have someone to stand by you and fight with you or to support you. What is this term?

20. This term comes from relay races, where a runner

carries an object up to a certain distance and then gives it to the next player, who then takes it on to the next. They are, thus, handing over their responsibility to someone else. The description of this action and the object involved gives rise to the term that is now used to describe a situation where a person hands over responsibility or duties to someone else.

ANSWERS

1. Southpaw
2. Grand Slam
3. The ball in their court
4. Stalemate
5. Googly
6. Caddie, golf
7. Hat-trick
8. Puck
9. Hands down
10. Duck, golden duck, diamond duck in cricket
11. Catching a crab
12. Football
13. Decoy
14. Volleyball
15. Slam dunk
16. Across the board

17. Saved by the bell

18. Hail Mary pass

19. Have someone in your corner

20. Pass the baton

14. FICTIONAL SPORTS

1. The Assassin's Guild Wall Game is a 'cross between squash, urban ____ _____ and actual bodily harm.' It is played in the fictional city of Ankh-Morpok by guild members where school houses have their own teams, and the teams compete against one another in climbing buildings, often done on unusual/notable buildings in the city itself, with each major building having a rating out of 10, representing how difficult it is to climb. The blanked-out name is that of an actual sport where participants climb up, down or across natural rock formations or artificial rock walls. The goal is to reach the summit of a formation or the endpoint of a usually pre-defined route without falling. What is the name of this actual sport which forms the basis of the Guild Wall Game?

2. Lifting is a popular fictional extreme sport from the Anime series Eureka Seven, where athletes ride 'reflection boards' on waves of 'Transparence Light

Particles (Trapar)'. Trapars are a particulate matter which behave much like water or strong wind currents. Lifting is based on an actual sport where athletes ride waves of another kind. They have 20–30 minutes to catch a wave and every wave they catch is rated on a ten-point scale by a panel of judges and only the two best waves of each athlete is counted, giving them a score on 20. What is this popular sport that has recently garnered a good following in India, especially in Chennai?

3. Anbo-Jitsu is a fictitious sport on a TV show where two armoured opponents facing each other wear a solid visor, rendering them blind, and fight with a large staff which contains a proximity sensor, alerting each contender to their opponent's location with an audio signal. It is called 'the ultimate evolution in the martial arts' in the context of the show. This show was a pioneering science fiction series which was telecast 1987 onwards. In which show did Anbo-Jitsu appear, where men, women and others boldly go where no one has gone before?

4. In *Avatar: The Legend of Korra* there is a fictional football/soccer/MMA hybrid sport where two teams utilize their respective elements in combat to push the other team back and gain territory on an elevated, six-sector, hexagonal field in a best-of-three-falls match. Players try to knock each other back or off the end of the field into the water pit below, and the team that wins two rounds achieves a 'knockout'. No member of

any team in the running for the championship may get into a physical confrontation with another player of an opposing team outside of a match. The name of the sport refers to the fact that it is the professional version of a person's ability to manipulate a specific physical element: water, earth, fire or air. What is this ability known as and what is the name of this sport?

5. 12 Ball is a game similar to four-player ping pong but played on a table shaped like a plus (+) with a player standing at each point and wielding two double ended paddles. A hand comes out of the middle, serves the ball and periodically adds more until there are 12 in play. This sport is usually played by a family which consists of three siblings with magical abilities. This family is at the centre of a fantasy teen situational comedy show from Disney which ran for five years. Which was this Emmy award winning show that launched the career of Selena Gomez?

6. In the book *Orbital Resonance* by John Barnes, the climax involves a variable-gravity sport where you have multiple teams and multiple mobile goals in microgravity. It is based on an actual team sport where players use a stick with a small net at the end to carry, pass, catch and shoot the ball into the goal. The name of the game is supposed to have come from the French word for 'the stick'. Considering that this fictional version is played in microgravity, its name is a portmanteau of the fact that it is played in air and the latter part of the actual sport. What is the name of

this sport invented by John Barnes?

7. This sport is an improvisational game that came about because the lead character of a very popular series had a bad experience when trying to join the school baseball team. It is a self-modifying game which is a contest of wits, skill and creativity rather than stamina or athletic skill. The only consistent rules are that the sport must never be played with the same rules twice and that each participant must wear a mask. Scoring is quite nonsensical with scores such as 'Q to 12' and 'oogy to boogy'. The absence of fixed rules causes issues between the participants as to who scored, where the boundaries are, and when the game is finished. The name of the sport is a portmanteau of the name of the lead character and name of the sport he had a bad experience with. What is the name of the sport?

8. In the sci-fi book *Border Guards* by Greg Egan, there is a sport where the aim is to shape the wave function of a quantum-mechanical 'ball' so that the probability of it being inside one of the goals rises above a set threshold. This is achieved by using the motion of the players to alter the energy spectrum of the wave function: when a player moves across the field, the energy that this action provides (or absorbs) enables transitions between certain modes of the wave function. The sport gets its name from the field of physics it uses and the actual sport it most closely resembles. What is this sport known as?

9. 'Fireball' is a fictional sport developed by two

roommates turned friends. The rules of the game are somewhat vague, but essentially involve throwing around a flaming tennis ball. One of the friends who is wearing oven gloves and has a fire extinguisher says 'all we need is a little lighter fluid'. They even have an Ultimate Fireball version which requires a bowling ball and a propane torch. Their other friend, who is completely unimpressed, calls the whole thing a 'crazy lawsuit game'. Who are these two friends who came up with this maniacal game?

10. *Look Around You* was a 2005 British television comedy series in which we met Scot Nolan and Bunny Gnowles, two Americans who have invented a new sport that is supposedly taking Pennsylvania by storm. It is a crossover between golf and tennis and the name of the sport is a portmanteau of the names of the two games. They are also working on another sport called Dencing, which involves throwing sabres at a bullseye board which the opponent is wearing. What is the name of the first sport and which two sports make up Dencing?

11. This is a fictional version of an actual sport that involves hitting plastic or wooden balls with a mallet through hoops embedded in a grass playing court, to a peg at the end of the court. The most famous tennis club in England in Wimbledon is actually called the All England Lawn Tennis and _____ Club and still has a lawn for that purpose. The fictional version of this game has players using flamingoes as mallets,

hedgehogs as balls and playing cards as hoops. What game are they playing and where would one find this fictional version?

12. This is the name of a fictional sport and also the name of the film in which it was introduced. The sport is invented when the lead characters are challenged to a game of basketball and they invent this game to be able to win against more athletic types. It soon gains popularity and becomes a national league sport. The game lasts for nine innings and is played between two teams of three players each. The player has to shoot a ball through the hoop and, if successful, must run through the bases. The name of the game (and the film) is a portmanteau of the names of the two games whose rules make up this fictional sport. What is its name?

13. Apopudobalia is a sport which was supposed to be an ancient Greco-Roman sport that anticipates modern soccer. It appears in a German encyclopaedia of classical scholarship called *Der Neue Pauly Enzyklopaedie der Antike*. The book says that the sport enjoyed a certain popularity amongst the Roman legions, and consequently spread throughout the empire. This sport is completely fictional and did not exist in any form whatsoever, and the name was completely made up. Why did the editors put this fictitious sport in the book?

14. This sport, which also shares its name with a 1975 film that revolves around it, consists of two teams

which can either be on roller skates or motorcycles, which compete to put a steel ball into goals located at opposite ends of an arena. The sport is made even more dangerous by the fact that because it takes place in an overpopulated dystopian world, athletes are encouraged to get rid of opponents permanently. What is the name of this horrifying fictional sport which is a portmanteau of the words for the means of transport and the entity they fight for?

15. This sport, which takes place on alien planets involves riding in a tiny cockpit which is tethered via cables to two massive jet engines. The participants have to try and overtake their opponents as they go through multiple laps of rocky terrain filled with giant obstacles at thousands of miles per hour. These events are projected in entertainment establishments throughout the galaxy. The film in which this sport appears revolves around the life of a slave who was the only human to have taken part in this and eventually won it as well. Who was this legendary character and what is this sport called?

ANSWERS

1. Rock climbing
2. Surfing
3. Star Trek
4. Bending, pro-bending
5. Wizards of Waverly Place

6. Aerocrosse (aero + lacrosse)

7. Calvinball

8. Quantum soccer

9. Chandler & Joey (from Episode 5.10, 'The One with the Inappropriate Sister')

10. Gonnis, darts + fencing

11. Croquet, *Alice in Wonderland*

12. Basketball

13. A copyright trap to ensure they could check up if anyone else had plagiarized their work

14. Rollerball

15. Anakin Skywalker, podracing

ACKNOWLEDGEMENTS

Berty and Akhila wish to thank their families for giving them an early exposure to and abiding passion for various sports.

Akhila: I would like to thank various members of my family, especially my parents who helped me stay up late at night to follow their (and then my) favourite sports and players and understood the gut-wrenching horror of watching your favourite player lose at 3.00 in the morning! My amazing cousins, who have such differing opinions and great insights into the game—and my grandparents.

One of my favourite sporting memories is my grandfather picking me up from school in the middle of a Test series between India and Australia at Eden Gardens and updating me on the day's scores and happening on the way home, before sitting down to watch it with my family. (Nobody knew then that the match would become legendary!) One grandmother follows tennis avidly and passed on her love of sports and athletics to her children (and grandchildren) and my other grandmother not only sat with me as I watched tennis and cricket but has learnt various other sports that her other grandchildren played. I would like to thank Berty Ashley for staying up late into the night so I could sob into the phone over the result of a cricket match and for being such amazing company at all matches and for sharing some crazy sports-fan ambitions! Finally, I'd like to thank my mother for helping me explore dance and martial arts and understanding the amazing feats the human body can accomplish, and my father for all the late nights and dawn matches and the text updates when I couldn't watch them, and the consolation as well as celebrations!